LAURA KRAUSS MELMED ◆ JIM LaMARCHE

The Rainbabies

LOTHROP, LEE & SHEPARD BOOKS   NEW YORK

For my parents—LKM   For my mother and father—JLM

First Edition   13 14 15 16 17 18 19 20
Library of Congress Cataloging in Publication Data
Melmed, Laura Krauss. The rainbabies / by Laura Krauss Melmed : illustrated by Jim LaMarche.
p.   cm.   Summary: When the moon gives twelve tiny babies to a childless couple, the new parents take great care of their charges and eventually receive
an unexpected reward. ISBN 0-688-10755-9. — ISBN 0-688-10756-7 (lib. bdg.) [1. Fairy tales.]   I. LaMarche, Jim, ill.   II. Title.   PZ8.M5214Rai 1992
[E]—dc20 91-16877 CIP AC

IN A SMALL HOUSE IN A GREEN MEADOW LIVED AN OLD WOMAN AND her husband of many years. Food they had aplenty and a good roof over their heads, and the river ran close to their door. But the thing they wanted most was the thing they lacked: a child to call their own.

The days of good honest work left little time for pining. But when twilight fell, the old woman would sit down at her table and sigh. "If children grew in flowerpots or blew down the chimney with the March wind, what a lucky woman I would be!"

One spring night, the couple was tucked in bed, snoring softly, when a broad ribbon of white light slid across the old woman's pillow. Her eyes flew open as she sat bolt upright. Though she could hear the steady tattoo of rainfall on the rooftop, her gaze met the white face of the full moon, peering round-mouthed through her window.

The old woman shook her husband. "Wake up, old man, I've heard the moonshower brings good fortune to everyone it touches!"

The old man rose, grumbling, and followed his wife outside. Though the shower had all but ended, the last drops of warm rain touched them. The old wife smiled and squeezed his hand. Then her eye caught a silvery glint in the meadow grass.

Bending down to get a better look, the woman gasped at what the moon revealed. Nestled among the wet blades of grass and the wildflowers were a dozen shimmering drops of water, each holding a tiny baby no larger than her big toe!

With utmost care, the couple gathered up the wee babies and brought them into the house. The woman dried them gently and set them on a soft cloth atop the kitchen table: twelve perfect little ones, all in a row.

The old couple smiled and cooed at the babies until they began to yawn and rub their eyes with tiny fists. Then the woman wrapped the rainbabies snugly in scraps of flannel and laid them to sleep in the dresser drawer. She and her husband, marveling at what had befallen them, returned to bed.

Day after day, the old couple cared for the rainbabies and soon grew accustomed to their ways. The infants seemed happiest after dusk and when the sky was overcast. When they were tired or wanted to be held, they cried out in tinkling voices and reached up with their plump little arms.

Then the old man and woman soothed the rainbabies in the palms of their hands, or rocked them to sleep in a pair of wooden shoes lined with handkerchiefs. The old woman would sing:

> Bye and bye, bye and bye,
> The moon is half a lemon pie,
> The mice who stole the other half
> Have scattered star crumbs in the sky.
>
> Bye and bye, bye and bye,
> My darling babies, don't you cry.
> The moon is still above the hill,
> The soft clouds gather in the sky.

On warm, hazy days, the old man and woman would carry the babies in a willow basket as they went about their chores. One cloudy morning the family set out with fishing poles in their wooden boat to catch some supper. The woman placed the basket at her feet.

The rainbabies were soon lulled to sleep by the gentle roll of the river. The old man and woman baited their hooks and dropped their fishing lines into the water.

No sooner had their hooks been swallowed by the river than the boat began to pitch. Seized by a powerful current, the boat was drawn into a foaming whirlpool. A mighty wave rose up and over the side of the boat, and before the old man and old woman could stop it, the basket of babies was swept overboard.

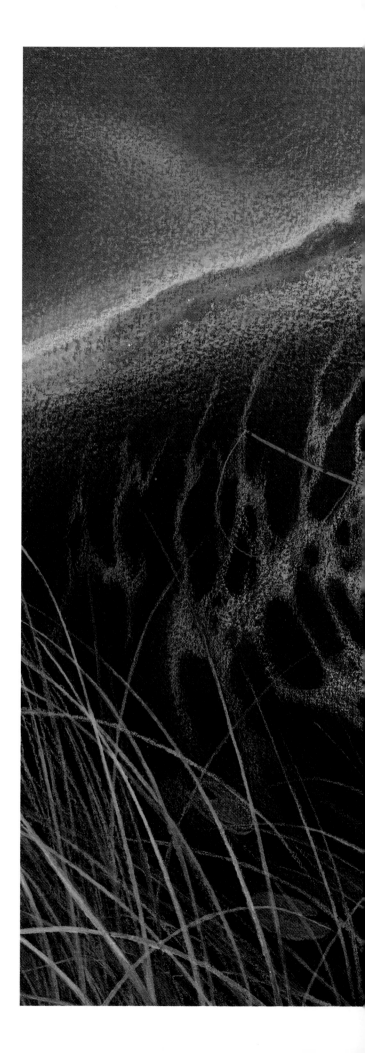

The old man plunged into the river. Round and round he swam, trying to reach the basket. He swam until his heart pounded like a hammer. His limbs burned as if they were on fire, although the water was cold.

Then a faint sound reached him over the roar of the current. He turned to see the old woman, gesturing wildly with a fishing pole. With a heave, she flung the pole, and the old man grabbed it.

Reaching out with it, he hooked the basket's handle. Then he drew
the basket to him and lifted it from the water. Instantly, the river
regained its calm.

The old man swam back to his wife, handed the basket up to her,
and climbed into the boat. Relieved, but wet and exhausted, the
couple embraced and rowed home, forgetting about their fish.

Some days later, the wind began to whip about the meadow.
"The peaches have ripened and should be picked, wife. Let us
gather them now, before the wind does our work for us," said the
old man.

So the old woman carried the basket of babies to the orchard and laid it in a small clearing. The old man climbed a ladder that was leaning against one of the gnarled trunks. He picked a peach and handed it carefully down to his wife.

Suddenly, the sky deepened to an iron gray, bathing the orchard in a bluish glow. A crash of thunder sounded as a bolt of lightning struck the ground close to the basket where the rainbabies were sleeping.

Flames quickly enclosed the clearing in a perfect ring of fire. The willow basket lay trapped inside, the rainbabies wailing.

The woman tore the apron from her waist and started beating the flames. But as quickly as she subdued them, they rose again. Seeing this, the old man leaped across the barrier of fire and seized the basket. Then he returned through the blaze. As he handed the basket to his wife, a sudden rush of cool rain extinguished the circle of fire. The rainbabies were unharmed.

The next day dawned blue as chicory. The husband went early to the river to fish. The wife went to work in the vegetable garden. Although the wild waters and the fire had made her fearful of taking the babies outdoors, she feared more to leave them alone in the house. So she laid them on a blanket in the broad shade of a chestnut tree.

A passing weasel spied the silvery-pink babies and mistook them for newborns of her own kind. A lucky mother, to have so many little

ones, she thought, and me with none to call my own! With so many mouths to feed, who would mind one missing?

The weasel approached the blanket, sniffing and prodding the babies with her long whiskery snout. But the babies, sensing danger, cried out. The old woman came running, still clutching a turnip freshly dug from the earth. She reached the blanket just in time to see the weasel bound off with a tiny rainbaby dangling from her mouth.

The old woman set off after them, stuffing the turnip in her pocket. Round and round the meadow ran the woman and the weasel, over hillocks and through brambles, until the woman's head began to spin and her aching legs told her they must soon give out.

Then she remembered the turnip in her pocket. She tossed it over
the weasel's head, hitting the ground in front of the startled animal.
The weasel dropped the frightened rainbaby and ran off. The old
woman snatched up the baby and returned to find the others waiting
safely in the shade.

That night, after a good supper of brown bread and chowder, the old couple sat nodding by the fire. Shadows of kettles and cooking spoons danced along the walls. The rainbabies slept soundly in their drawer.

A loud knock roused the old man. As he pulled the door open, a strong blast of cold air and rain rushed into the kitchen, almost sweeping him from his feet. Over the threshold stumbled a tall figure wrapped in a heavy cloak.

The old couple watched open-mouthed as the strange figure threw off his hood, revealing the face of a handsome youth, his cap pulled securely over his hair. He strode across the room and placed on the table a basket woven from silvery twigs. Its white velvet cover was embroidered with tiny pearls.

The old woman gathered her wits. "Who are you?" she asked.

"I am a messenger, sent by Lady Coeur de Claire, a woman of vast and incredible riches," replied the young man. He pulled an object from his cloak. Suspended between his thumb and forefinger on a chain of spun silver, it swung slowly in the firelight: a gleaming white jewel, the size and shape of a hen's egg. The couple stared.

"Though my lady has enormous wealth," continued the messenger, "in one thing she is poor: she has been blessed with

neither sons or daughters, and for these she yearns beyond yearning. Therefore, she offers you this precious moonstone in exchange for the twelve babies in your charge. Give her the babies and live your remaining days in comfort and riches, for the moonstone is worth many sacks of gold coins."

The old woman moved closer to the sleeping rainbabies.

"Thank you," she said, "but the babies will stay with us."

The old man put his arm around her shoulder.

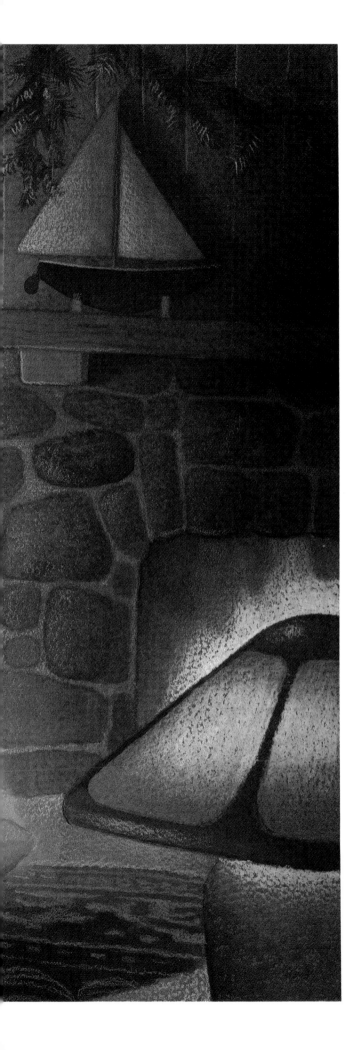

"So be it," said the youth.

He slipped the silver chain over his head. No sooner had the moonstone touched his chest than the cloak and cap fell away, and in his place appeared a woman of breathtaking beauty.

"My dear old man and woman," she said, "I am Mother Moonshower. On the night of the last full moon, I gave my rainbabies into your care.

"What loyal and loving caretakers you have been! You protected them from dangers born of water, fire, and earth. You refused the offer of great riches to keep the babies with you. You have proven yourselves the worthiest of parents. But now I have come to take the rainbabies away with me."

"You mustn't!" the old woman exclaimed.

"Please understand," said Mother Moonshower, "the rainbabies cannot grow properly without me. I will cherish them as you did. And do not fear—I will not leave you lonely. See what I have brought for you!"

She beckoned them to the table, where the silver basket lay all but forgotten, and lifted the cover.

Inside the basket lay the most beautiful baby girl the old couple had ever seen. She had hair like the midnight sky, and she smiled up at them with shining gray eyes.

As the man lifted the little girl in his arms, Mother Moonshower scooped the rainbabies into the basket.

"Wait!" cried the old woman. She bent to the silver basket, touching her lips softly to the forehead of each sleeping rainbaby. Each one smiled in turn without waking. As the woman kissed the last tiny brow, Mother Moonshower and the rainbabies disappeared.

The couple named their daughter Rayna. Like all children, she brought her parents great joy, and a bit of heartache too, but never such adventures as had befallen the rainbabies. Growing stronger

and more lovely with each passing year, Rayna picked the sweetest
peaches from the orchard and caught the sleekest fish. Her laughter
warmed the small house.

Some nights, when the full moon shone, the couple stood at the window. They watched their daughter, arms outstretched and hair floating in the soft breeze, whirling gracefully across the moonlit meadow.

And the old couple felt themselves truly fortunate, for their happiness was complete.